CHILDRENZ TWO

Stories for 12-16 years.

Selected and edited

by

Jill Darragh

Rangitawa
PUBLISHING

Childrenz Two first published 2014.

Published by Rangitawa Publishing, Feilding, New Zealand.

Copyright Jill Darragh 2014.

www.rangitawapublishing.com

rangitawa@xtra.co.nz

ISBN 978-9941088-0-7

From the Editor

This is the second selection of stories entered in the Rangitawa Publishing 'Write a Children's Story' competition 2014.

Childrenz One is a collection suitable for readers of 8-11 years old. **Childrenz Two** comprises of stories for readers aged 12 -16.

The writer's ages in this book range from eleven years old to adult. I would like to thank all the authors who supported this project.

Please note that all due care has been taken to ensure there are no errors in this book but if readers find a mistake they are welcome to contact me and I will correct the file for future readers.

Jill Darragh 2014

Contents

A BIRD'S EYE VIEW OF A TRUE STORY

By Rebecca de Klerk age 15   (1st prize)

The first thing I remember is light. Bright wonderful light. For a chick, this is actually quite unusual, as chicks are supposed to hatch under a hen. In normal cases then, a chick's first memories should be of darkness, shouldn't it?

Anyway you may wonder why I remember light if I hatched under a hen, but to tell the truth I have never seen either of my parents, they died before I hatched. Now this may seem impossible, parents dying before you are born, but believe it or not, it's true! Here is my story, and as far as I am concerned it starts before the beginning. Well, before my beginning.

My Father was called The Fat Controller. No one knew his real name and no one knew where he had come from. He was just there, living in amongst the trees in a small hilly paddock inhabited by horses. The Fat Controller was a handsome young Pekin rooster, who wore a beautiful pair of trousers, had a bright red comb and wattles, smart orange waistcoat, and a lovely greeney blue tail.

I am afraid to say The Fat Controller was of a vain disposition, and considered himself to be an extremely accomplished singer, giving renditions of his fine vocal chords every morning and evening. The Fat Controller was quite friendly with the people who owned the horses.

Every day they fed the horses a bucket of warm feed, and since horses are rather messy eaters, they generally spilt a lot of their dinner. The Fat Controller's beady eyes noticed this fact, and when the horses thought they were finished, he would scurry in to polish off the fallen crumbs. Sometimes, when the people were feeling especially kind, they would give The Fat Controller his favourite treat: a bruised banana!

One day, the people felt sorry for The Fat Controller, because he was all alone. They thought and thought about what could be done, and eventually hit on a solution. They decided it was high time that The Fat Controller had a wife, and made arrangements the very next day.

When the people came to his paddock with a box, The Fat Controller, being of an inquisitive nature, hurried over to investigate. The box was opened and from it was lifted the most beautiful hen The Fat Controller had ever seen! She was covered in black and white stripes, her eyes were beady bright and oh! The Fat Controller gasped, she was a Pekin just like him, and she too had a pair of fluffy trousers!

Quite carried away by this vision of loveliness, The Fat Controller's chest swelled with self importance. Without waiting for introductions, he strutted up to the beautiful stranger and did a little dance designed to impress. The Lady, very offended by such bold manners, was so shocked, she decided to ignore The Fat Controller. When he offered her some juicy grubs, she pretended not to notice. Chicken Little, for that was her name, decided she would go and explore her new surroundings and leave this uncouth stranger to his own devices.

As it was getting dark Chicken Little flew up into the branches of a low tree and settled down for the night. Sleep would not come to Chicken Little though, and she spent a long and scary night filled with strange noises and dark shadows. When at last the sun peeped over the hills, Chicken Little was in such a state she completely forgot her resolve to ignore the strange character she had met the day before. At that very moment she heard a beautiful tenor voice raised in song, and looking down, she saw The Fat Controller.

Suddenly realizing how very handsome he was, she flew down to join him. After a few happy weeks together, Chicken Little laid nine small white eggs in a hollow under a fallen tree, and lined her nest with her own soft downy feathers. The Fat Controller almost burst with pride at the thought of chicks, and stood close by to guard his wife and growing family.

But alas, tragedy struck the newlyweds only a few days later. Death stalked The Fat Controller and his wife in the shape of a weasel. The Fat Controller fought valiantly to defend his wife, but no chicken is a match for a weasel, however brave he is.

A blood red sun arose over the hills and the eggs lay abandoned, the only sign of The Fat Controller were a few scattered feathers. But those eggs did not follow their unfortunate parents. Before they grew too cold, the people who owned the horses discovered the deserted nest with its precious bundle inside. They quickly and carefully gathered the pearly eggs and hurried them home to an incubator.

So there you have the answer to why I was hatched in light. The people bestowed me with the grand title of Perigrin Chook, and named my sister Meriadoc Brandycluck, Pippin and Merry for short.

I would not recommend being raised by humans to every chick, as it leads to a rather conceited view of oneself. My sister Merry also had a sad tendency to be pugnacious.

As I grew into a handsome young cockerel I discovered early one morning I had not only inherited my father's looks, a glossy red waistcoat and dark green tail, but also his fine talent for singing. I am sorry to say that I took every opportunity to show off my voice, even in the middle of the night. This inexcusable behaviour of mine led to my downfall.

I have never understood humans, and I don't expect you to try, but believe it or not, some humans complained about my vocal chords! The Council gave me one week to pack my bags, kiss good-bye to my many wives and dozens of kids, and move out.

And guess what? I was relocated to the very same hill in the very same paddock that my father had lived and died in! I was given a smart little hutch to live in, and for company two wives, imaginatively called Red and Orange.

Living on a tree covered hill with two wives and a smart hutch isn't all that bad. For many months we lived happily enjoying our idyllic life in the country. We discovered a beautiful bowl of dust, and spent delightful hours bathing there. There were interesting logs to explore, an abundance of tasty grubs and insects, and wonderful shelter when it was raining. I was quite content. We kept in touch with the family back home via the sparrows who would carry any message for a small portion of our breakfast.

I learned that Merry was raising her fourth brood of chicks, and Cinnamon, a pretty partridge coloured Pekin, was going broody for the second time. I also discovered, to my great joy, I was a Grandrooster! My son, Sherlock Combs, and his wife Lacewing had hatched out a young cock chick and called him Peepybird (not exactly Hercules is it!).

All this chick-talk went to Red's head, and she decided to raise her own family. She found a dry nesting site hidden away under a small bush and sat tight on her collection of eggs. That night I went to bed as usual with Orange, and we were locked up snugly in our hutch. In the morning when I went to visit Red, she was gone. All her precious eggs were stone cold, the small life within each one snuffed out. A few red feathers was all that remained and a dark, evil smell. I vowed to protect Orange at all costs, even with my life, if necessary.

A few days later we snuggled down for the night in our hutch. Unbeknown to us, the door of our hutch was accidentally left open. Silver moonlight shone down on a dark shape creeping towards the open door...

This is where I, Meriadoc Brandychook, take up quill to record the following events. I learned from the sparrows the fate of my brother Pippin. Death had stolen my brother away, the same as my father and mother. The people found a few feathers and the one last egg Orange had ever laid. They gave the egg to Cinnamon and she faithfully promised to raise the life within.

Three weeks later a chick hatched out, born after her parents had died. Cinnamon called her Tweety Bird. It seemed at first that my brother's life had been wasted, that he had lived and died with no one to remember him, but then I looked around. In the shade of the loquat tree Lacewing was teaching Peepybird to dust bathe, Cinnamon was showing Tweety Bird how to eat worms, and around me, my own children sat, enjoying the sun. I realized that although I would never see Pippin again, he was not gone. He was here, living through his children, and that as long as they and their descendents lived, he would never be forgotten.

Idiots in Space

By William Wood age 12. (2nd prize)

Warning at the start of this story there will be a test; do you wish to go on?

You obviously do because you're reading this. Well done you've passed the test. What was the test you ask? Knowing how to read of course, if you didn't know how to read you couldn't read this therefore you would have failed duh.

Now on more pressing matters, the 121st issue of *Idiots Guide To Space*. In this edition of *Idiots Guide To Space* I will be telling you what to do with a cosmic snail, where the letter P comes from, how to tell what planet you're on, and the secrets of time travel.

So it seems that you are interested in finding out what to do with a Cosmic Snail (or you're bored and just need something to read, or on an off chance that for some reason you're reading this for a short story competition that a boy has entered). Either way you're reading this and you're going to find out about a cosmic snail.

A cosmic snail has a shiny black shell with small white dots on it to help disguise it-self if it were to be floating in deep space. Unfortunately the cosmic snail's natural planet is completely white, so its camouflage actually makes it stand out more. If/when you find a cosmic snail you should remember to pick it up by the shell because if you don't it will hate you and not invite you to its exclusive party. If you do though it will love you. Now that you have a cosmic snail that likes you, you should do the same to approximately six million more snails then you will have an army of snails that love you. Use your army of snails to take over whatever planet you want.

How will the snails take over you ask? Instruct your snails to create singing bubbles. The cosmic snail's only defense is to create slime trails that release bubbles that sing, their song is beautiful but with that many at once the sound would be deafening. (You probably should wear John's high quality ear muffs).

Now to where the letter P comes from. There have been many great lies told that someone just came up with the letter but in fact it was actually found. Yes I'm saying that letter P was dropped off on the side of the road by a strange man in a truck. The letter P cried in the ditch for a while before he was adopted by the alphabet. Before the letter P was adopted the *alphabet* was just called the *alhabet*, because the original *alphabet* was founded by a guy called *Al Habet*. The letter has revolutionized the alphabet and now days it is a well-respected letter living in a mansion on the planet Zircon. Now you know where the letter comes from you should tell friends/acquaintances/business friends/business partners/children/wife/local hobo/random people on the street the truth about P.

Now I'm going to give you a break to: get a cup of coffee, or go and take over a planet with snails, you know that sort of thing...

Did you have a good break? Then again I'm a story so I can't tell if you did or didn't, but anyway. I'm now up to telling you what planet you're on.

Now before we start you need to know who Pluto the barking dog is (off Mickey Mouse 2000). We'll start off with something you know, if you find a cosmic snail you're on Blandis, the completely bland and white planet. Earth now days are one of the biggest intergalactic trade routes in the universe so you should quite easily know that. You should know if you're on a sun because you will be on fire burning to death, if you are on a sun right now reading this then I'm probably going to be destroyed with you so my only regrets are that I never told my mum I was still alive I just couldn't be bothered to ring her, I regret that I never became a multi billionaire, and finally I regret that I was bought from a lower class gas station by you not some rich person who collects every issue and keeps me in perfect condition in a display box.

Well I guess that you weren't on a sun because you would be dead by now so thanks, any way back to the planets.

Now to Pluto, all you have to do is feel around all the trees...... BARK! Even we short stories have a sense of humor, you know because dogs bark and stuff... yeah you get it. Now since there are 542,666,785,962,589 planets in the universe it would take approximately 100 bajillion million gazillion years to tell you about them all so I have prepared a song to help. Ifffff youuu knew aboutttt all theeee 542 trillion 666 billion 785 million 962 thousand 589 planeeeeets in theee uniiiiiiverseeee it would take approximatelyyyyy 100 bajillion million gazillion yearsssss. I know it needs a chorus.

I'm now going to tell you all the deep and dark secrets of time travel. It has always been a big secret where the power for time travel comes from. A time machine gets its energy from an unknown source, although many people have claimed to have heard puffing after they time travel. Now a time machine takes you back in time but in the same place so before you travel you need to know what was there 500 million years ago (or however many years you are going back) to make sure that you're not going to end up in the middle of a mountain or something.

Now I am here to explain the unexplained and I am going to break down lies and bring forth the truth (I thought that sounds like something a hero would say). Anyway I'm going to explain the panting that people hear after time travel, but I won't tell you just yet.   A time machine has a huge area underneath the floor but no one knows what it's for. Well it's actually where the machine gets its power from, the rooms full of gym equipment attached to small wires that all connect into one really, really big wire that goes out of the room into the engine. There are also lots and lots of mini houses with small potato people living in them that come out and run on the treadmills. Yes I'm telling the truth time travel is powered by small, running, potatoes. Hey I never said that the guy who invented the time machine sane, but he was brilliant; he knew that the race of small running potatoes were obsessed with fitness.

Now that I am done with telling you about: cosmic snails, the letter P, planets, and time travel I'm going to have to leave you. Thank you, thank you, you've been a lovely audience, please, please no autographs, I'll see you next week, bye.

Geek chic

By Evie Sanson age 12 (3rd prize)

"Dad I'm home."

I throw my bag on the couch and walk into the kitchen.

"Oh hello honey did you have a nice day?"

Dad and Steve are standing in the kitchen looking at each other in their special way. When they are looking at each other like that the world could explode and they wouldn't notice.

"Dad, Dad I think something's burning!"

He snaps out of the daze and pulls a cookie sheet from the oven. "Surprise I made your favourite vegan peanut brownies."

Yep as well as having a gay Dad I'm a vegan and a self-confessed geek. I reach out to grab a cookie but Steve taps my hand, I place it by my side.

"Steve!"

"You have to wait a few minutes for them to cool."

I walk over to the tea box. All I can see is green tea.

"Dad have we got any peppermint tea?"

"Did you have a bad day again?"

"Yeah, oh by the way Alex is coming over tonight."

Dad walks off and starts to make a cup of peppermint tea. Alex is the only other geeky vegan that I know. We met in the library when I was six I had found a hole in the shelves that I could just fit through, one day I went to crawl into my safe space Alex was sitting there. And that's where our awkward friendship began.

At exactly 6:00 Alex arrives. Dad and Steve have gone out to their annual Gay and Lesbian Society meetings. Alex and I have a light dinner of green bean salad and green tea. Then we watch our favourite show Big Bang Theory. Then we talk about our math homework. When Dad and Steve get home Alex leave.

"So did he ask you to prom?"

"No, you know that we are strictly friends."

"Well, is there someone that you want to go with?"

I look at Dad with my signature 'don't even go there look'. " Awkward" Steve suddenly calls out.

It's at times like these that I don't mind having two Dads. Dad opens up the tin of peanut brownies. I grab two and go off to my room to work on my dress for prom. Last year I found the perfect fabric for my dress; it is a light teal colour with a white Eiffel tower print. Every night I sew a bit of it.

The next day at school Liam from my science class asks me to prom. I practically skip home. Steve comes home and takes about five minutes to snap me out of my daze. I immediately tell him the good news.

On the days that lead up to prom I am so excited. Liam leaves notes in my locker and flowers in my desk. One day, as I'm returning the books that I got out about dress making, I bump into Alex.

"Why are you going with Liam?"

"Um... cause I like him and he asked me."

"You like him?"

"Yeah I suppose so."

Alex just storms off.

On the night of the prom I take my dress out of the cupboard, it is really beautiful. Dad gently knocks on my bedroom door.

"Wow you look amazing."

"You really think so?"

"Yeah, anyway Liam is here. Have a great time."

Liam went all out, a teal rose corsage with gold flecks and a stretched limo. When we arrive at the dance Liam says he has something to tell me. He takes me out of the hall and says, "I don't want you to be my date."

"But you asked me."

"No, it was a bet made by my friends. I won so um, yeah if you could get one of your Dads to pick you now that would be great."

I run away crying. After half an hour or so Alex comes and finds me sitting alone.

"What's the matter?"

"Nothing just guys breaking my heart that kind of stuff."

I look up Alex is in a tux with no hair gel in his hair, he looks good.

"Um isn't your eye stuff meant to be all down your face because you've been crying."

"No cause if you use water proof eye stuff that doesn't happen."

"Oh ok."

I call Dad and he comes and gets me and Alex. When we get home we see that Dad and Steve have been working hard they've made a mini prom for us. They must have got out of Christmas decorations because there are fairy lights everywhere, and tinsel over everything.

"We still wanted the night to be magical, so we set this up for you."

Dad and Steve dance together all night. Alex sleeps on the couch. By the time the first rays of the morning are appearing I start to realise that even though Liam broke my heart, Alex has mended it.

Over time our relationship has gone from friends to couple. Finally after we both got our PHDs, Alex proposed to me and Dad and Steve died an old happy couple.

Camping

By Hannah Evans age 12

The sun was going down, fire burning strongly. Everyone was happy. The smell of marshmallows wafted up my nose as I inhaled a breath of fresh clean air.

It was the start of the school holidays. My family had been planning an overnight tramp in the bush for what seemed like months, even years to me. Finally it had been put into reality so I was going to take in every single aspect of it.

My two annoying older brothers Maverick and Paddy were playing around with the rugby ball near the river, while Mum and Dad were sitting on a log sharing stories.

I finished eating all the sweet marshmallows I wanted then went over to see our family's Jack Russell puppy 'Alfie'. Alfie was curled up in a tiny ball on top of my bright Fluoro pink and orange sleeping bag that Granny had gifted to me a few years ago. She told me that I had to look after it and I did although I thought the bag was completely hideous.

Alfie was twitching in his sleep. I sat with him thinking about my Granddad who died two years ago yesterday. It seemed as if I was the only person in the world who had remembered. I looked down at the golden locket that was hanging around my neck. I carefully opened making sure that I didn't break it.

Inside there was an old faded photo of him when he was about my age or a little younger maybe only ten years of age. On the other side of the golden heart with was a tiny photo of Granddad holding me when I was a baby.

For a split second I stared into the distance. The bush was silent and the sound of birds overwhelmed me. This is paradise. Away from the bustle of people on the streets, away from the cars speeding down the flat endless streets, away from the city lights. This was different for me, but I loved it. I soon felt tired and fell asleep.

Next morning I woke up before dawn. Mum was up, starting to cook pancakes. I knew from experience how long it takes her to make them so I decided to go for a little walk while I waited.

I hadn't gone far when Alfie raced out from nowhere nearly knocking me over. As I regained my balance he leaped through a bush and then was gone. I didn't think twice and leaped through after him. I ran and ran and ran. He just wouldn't stop chasing what he was after no matter how hard I called for him.

"ALFIE, ALFIE, ALFIE." I screamed at the top of my lungs.

He was beginning to slow down when I realised that I had been running for a long time, at least an hour. Alfie stopped and looked at me with a worried look. That was when I knew I was lost. I was in the middle of the bush, all by myself. No compass, no GPS. Nothing. That was it. I had given up hope.

I sat on a mossy log and stared at the ground. If only, if only, if only. Then I remembered it; the story that Granddad had told me when he handed the locket to me.

"I was out on a walk in the bush when I got lost. I don't remember how as it was when I was only little. Maybe your age or a little bit younger. I was with all of my friends. See, there I am on the trip."

He showed me one of the photos inside the locket.

"I knew I would never be able to get out by walking every which way so I thought for a bit. We had set up camp next to the river as it was then nice and easy to get water. So what I did was found the closest river and followed my instinct which was to walk down stream. I had been walking for maybe about forty five minutes when someone shouted at me 'Gary you're back. Have a nice walk?' All I want you to do with this knowledge is put it at the back of your head and hopefully you won't have to use it, but you never know."

I knew what I would have to do. Like Granddad had done we had camped next to the river so I listened hard for a faint sound of water. Sure enough there was a sound of a river. I walked slowly listening hard towards the sound. Alfie followed at my ankles seeming to know that he was the one that had got us into trouble.

Soon we reached the river. It was clear. I went to touch it. I gave a little scream. It was so cold it stung the tip of my finger! I decided to follow the river downwards. It seemed like I had been walking for hours when I saw a glimpse of something hanging between two big trees. One part of me was saying "Those are my togs" where as another part of me was saying "You're seeing things girl!!!"

I walked towards them when I heard a shriek. It was Mum. "What took you so long? You had me so worried. I thought you were lost. Do you know where Alfie is?"

"Slow down Mum," I said as calmly as I could. "Alfie came with me. We are both fine. We just had a little play around that's all and then we lost track of... ummmm...... time!"

In the evening the whole family kept asking me about what had happened. I didn't dare to tell them the whole truth as I wanted to come back for another holiday in the bush.

My new favourite thing is camping.

TIME FLIES

By Petra Gleridis

The Eagle's eye was warm and quiet and a little bit dark. The Venetian blinds covering the windows were still drawn and the only light that pervaded it came from the skylight.

Ellie was sleeping in puffy blankets just like the sneaking clouds, leaving their footprints on Ellie's face. She smiled in her dream and turned over. The other occupants of the Eagle's eye were also sleeping – her cello in the corner, her dad's microscope on the desk, her own telescope and the laboratory glassware her Dad didn't need any more.

Ellie had the gift to dream whatever she wanted and she often dreamed of flying with her cello or inside a Petri dish. Although still only twelve and seven months old, she was excellent at music and science. And it couldn't be otherwise as her Mum was the best piano and cello teacher in the town and her Dad resembled a weird scientist from a famous film– he invented, created, constructed, improved and modified lots of things and according to Ellie he had also been working on a time machine...

So Ellie could play the piano and the cello equally well; she adored the tiny things, seen under a microscope; the huge ones, seen through a telescope; and the invisible and the indivisible ones – the atoms. She had already had her own inventions such as tiramisu – flavoured cleaning tooth gum, lasagne – flavoured chewing gum, chocolate – flavoured chewing gum for sore throat, to name but a few.

"Weigh cup, weigh cup! Time to weigh the cup. Your time flies, Ellie, weigh cup!" blared the alarm.

Ellie had received it for her eleventh birthday from Mum and Dad and her Dad had made it especially for her. The thing was a tangle – haired gnome, as big as a small TV, jumping on a spring up and down. It was holding a cup which showed the time, the temperature and the atmospheric pressure in all time zones. It also displayed the exact time when the sun and the moon rose and set. The gnome could also tell the time in sixty - five languages, including in the endangered Chamicuro, Dumi and Ongota; he could do sums and serve as a computer as well. He had speech, smell and mood recognition software, which enabled him to hear whatever Ellie wanted to search in his data, to smell and recognize who the person was and tell exactly how he or she felt.

Ellie turned over and opened one eye. To weigh the cup...The gnome wouldn't stop jumping and urging Ellie out of her bed unless she got up and took the cup from its hands and placed it on the scales on its head. The procedure was so complex that one should be in a real awoken state to manage to perform the above steps.

"Weigh cup, weigh cup..." the gnome was still repeating his song.

Ellie was now sitting, trying to remember if it was Wednesday or Friday. For months she had been exhausted and craved for rest and.."

"Weigh cup..."

Ellie didn't touch the gnome, let alone its cup because she remained still for a second then started dancing around and singing. Soon she was jumping in unison with the gnome because she had remembered that it was actually Saturday which meant the first day of the summer holidays. It also meant that her parents were on their usual Saturday trip and all she had to do is enjoy herself all day long!

Still beaming, Ellie took the cup off the gnome's hands and weighed it on its head. The display on the cup showed a really strange message:

"Добро утро. Часът е 8:15. Слънцето изгрява в 05:16 и залязва в 20:37. Луната изгрява в 04:38 и залязва в 16:19. Навън е 25°C, а атмосферното налягане е ..."

Ellie hadn't come across such a language up that moment. Her gnome had already greeted her in Japanese, Chinese, Korean, Greek, Armenian, Georgian, but this one... She automatically pressed the key for translation, which was inside the gnome's ear. And the cup displayed:

"Good morning. The time is 8:15. The sun rises at 05:16 am and sets at 08:37 pm. The moon rises at 04:38 am and sets at 04:19 pm. It's25°C outside, the atmospheric pressure is..."

"What language is this?"

"Bulgarian. It is an Indo – European language..."

"OK, spare me the details. I suppose it's spoken in Bulgaria."

"Yes. Bulgaria is a country in south – eastern Europe. To the north it is bordered by Romania..."

"Count Dracula was Romanian. Just tell me the interesting facts, please. You know I hate history."

"Asparukh of Bulgaria ruled the Bulgar orda, reached the river Danube, defeated the Byzantine Emperor and established the first Bulgarian state in 681 AD. The first Bulgarian flag was a horse tail on a pole. The Bulgars shaved their heads, leaving several locks of hair, resembling the horse tail because the animal was sacred for them. They shaved their horse tails as well, they drank mare's milk and hardly dismounted their horses."

"Awesome!"

"Krum the Fearsome..."

"I know him from Harry Potter. He was the seeker for..."

"No, Krum the Fearsome or Khan Krum ruled in the 8th century and after killing the Byzantine emperor Nicephorus I in the Battle of Pliska, ordered a jeweled cup to be made from his skull from which he and his nobles drank while celebrating their victory."

"Brr, fearsome."

"Simeon I the Great made Bulgaria the most powerful state in Europe in 9th century and led its greatest territorial expansion ever - during his rule the country spread over the Aegean, the Adriatic and the Black Sea. His reign was a period of prosperity and enlightenment and was called the Golden Age of Bulgarian culture."

"Nice. Where are Mum and Dad?"

"Out."

"I know, but where?"

"Far behind."

"Far behind what?"

"Far behind us. They..."

Ellie wasn't listening. She knew all that would follow would be really ambiguous and incomprehensible. Besides, she had already been used to the gnome's way to interpret the facts sometimes and didn't want to go any further and find out what exactly he had in mind.

She had taken a piece of her favourite cleaning tooth gum, sitting on her bed in the lotus position and staring at her cello. There was something about it that she couldn't specify what. Finally she stood up and went closer it. There was a scratch on the tailpiece, which almost made her angry but she soon realized it was a word. Something was etched in tiny silver words.

Ellie took a magnifying glass but the words were still difficult to be read. She tried the zoom of her camera – still nothing. Then tore a piece of paper, put it over the word and with a black pencil slowly started to cover the piece. She knew that way the words would appear as if printed and she would be able to see them somehow. After the piece was dark, she attached it on a slide and put it under the microscope. Her heart was pounding with excitement as she was bending over and looking through the eye- lens. Ellie nearly fainted. Four tiny silver words were smiling at her and said: " *time.*"

Ellie came back to the cello and started inspecting it – she touched the scroll, the pegs, she tried the nut, the fingerboard, knocked on the top, pulled the strings, peeped in the F – holes, touched the tailpiece again and again, checked the sides, the neck, the back. Nothing.

Ellie repeated several times the word, thought what it might mean and didn't come up with anything reasonable. On repeating it for the forty-ninth time Ellie looked at the gnome. His wake – up song clearly appeared in her mind and she closed her eyes. Of course! How foolish she had been! Her Dad had made her a time machine and she needed exactly one year and seven months to perceive it. The gnome had been giving her the clue since her eleventh birthday: "Your time flies." Yes, her time, her cello…But how? The gnome…The message was in Bulgarian, the information was about the country centuries ago, then Mum and Dad…

"Are Mum and Dad in Bulgaria?"

"Yep."

"Have they been time travelling every Saturday?"

"Yep. Now listen to your dad's message:

Hello Kitten Ellie! Congratulations! We were sure today would be the day! You've solved the mystery and yes, you needed time. Fly to us. We are waiting for you.

Fly to them? But how? How did the machine work? Ellie had never been so nervous in her life. To calm down she took the bow and started playing. Slowly, slowly. Still concentrated on how to travel in time, she played her three favourite studies, then two short sonatas and just preparing to start another piece when… she froze. Literally. Half of the hair of her bow had fallen off. She looked at it – the heel was still holding several hairs but their ends were loose in the wind. In the wind? Ellie looked around and noticed she wasn't in her room – she was in a field, on a river bank, there were lots of strangely – looking people. All of them were shaven with a tail at the back of their heads. And the horses…She hadn't seen so many horses together. So many horses with shaven tails!

Ellie screamed as a horseman was approaching her, galloping. The rider didn't notice neither her, nor her cello or the shredding bow. Two other horses came nearer - one of the horsemen was holding a pole with horse tail fastened to its upper end. Ellie looked at her bow again and it did look like the Bulgars' first flag, the gnome had mentioned. The Bulgars?! So she had managed! She had travelled fourteen centuries back and had arrived in Bulgaria! But where were Mum and Dad? Now she saw them – they were waving and shouting, obviously they had already known that nobody could see or hear them.

"Hey, Kitten Ellie! You are here, at last!"

Mum was kissing her and holding her tightly in her arms. Dad also hugged and kissed her and then Ellie noticed that Dad had a bag made of an animal skin in his right hand that was giving off a strange smell, just as his breath.

"What's this? What do you smell of?"

"Oh, I drank a little mare's milk. I think it's a bit stale but I like it. Want to try?"

"No, thanks. Mum, where's your cello?"

"My cello? At home. Why?"

"How did you arrive then? Isn't your cello also a time machine?"

"Ellie, your Mum was humming her favourite sonata and I thought of protein biosynthesis and post-translational modification in particular. You came here by playing the cello because thus you relax and get rid of what worries you. To travel in time people don't need machines – all they need is in them. It's their willpower and imagination. You can put on a pair of sunglasses or use your favourite lip balm and arrive where you want. But you can't do anything without the determination to do it. I could have written *'time'* on a Petri dish or a volumetric flask, on the microscope or on the window and had the same success. It was you that made the travelling possible, your strong willpower to follow and find us. Music was only the background."

"Dad, do you know? You're a genius!"

"Kitten Ellie, I am a genius and I met Mum, who is also a genius and we had you – a square genius! Now, I think you need some horse hairs for your bow. Over there just a horse tail is being shaven. Then I think we should be going because I'm dying to drink wine from a human skull."

"And, honey, I think we should also go to the 9th century because I heard Simeon I the Great was really handsome."

"Hey!"

Journalist

By Gabi Harpur age 12

As I speed walked down the dingy alleyway clutching my state-of-the-art camera to my chest I peeked round the corner, panting.

"Gosh!" I thought. "They definitely weren't lying when they said that being a journalist is very good exercise!"

As I looked for my co-worker, Michelle I heard a loud bang from behind me. Another car bomb.

There have been lots of these recently each killing more and more innocent bystanders. Never mind about Michelle – she would know where I was. As I sprinted over to the scene of the tragedy I looked in horror at the result of this blast, bodies everywhere scattering the ground like litter. Who could want to do such a thing? Not bothering with the scoop on this hideous event I rushed over to the nearest person desperate to help which turned out to be a mother crying over what I presumed was her daughter.

"Can I help you?" I asked her in a panic.

"Call an ambulance please," she pleaded with me.

"What is your emergency?" said the operator.

"There has been a car bomb on the west side of the city," I tell her.

"We are aware of that event and we are sending several

ambulances over to you, do not panic."

"Ok," I replied.

After I hung up I told the panic-stricken mother that there was help coming. She thanked me profusely telling me I was her saviour. The ambulances soon came to the scene and took the girl and her mother away to the hospital but not before the mother told me to visit her which I planned on doing anyway.

As I walked into the make-shift hospital what greeted me was a scene of utter chaos, people running around yelling, doctors carrying clipboards and people silently crying next to someone. It was then that I realised the severity of the damage done – words do not describe the picture in front of me.

I made my way slowly down the aisle I searched for the girl and her Mum. When I found them the girl was sitting up and talking; it turns out she had just suffered a mild concussion but the doctors considered she would recover well physically. After chatting with them for several hours I found out that the mother's name was Raaghen (Ra-jen) and the daughter's name is Dereask (Dee-ask) and Raaghen's husband had been killed in the fighting in Afghanistan and that without the income they had to lose their home and were now living in Raaghen's sister's house. I also told them my name, Heather.

As I strolled out of the "hospital" I wondered what I could do to help these people... I could give them some money! Yes, that is what I could do! But, how would I get the funds together? Afterwards I pondered over that until I got back to the room where I was staying. It was then that I realised that I could go back to England and fundraise there.

A week later...

Grasping my plane tickets in my hands so I could not misplace them, I made my way to Terminal 2.

"Calling all passengers flying to Heathrow on flight 204 terminal 2 to board now, calling all passengers flying to Heathrow on flight 204 terminal 2 to board now," came the announcement.

This is it. The well-being of these suffering people lay in my hands. Looking out of the window towards the rugged terrain I fell into a peaceful, dreamless sleep.

I awoke to someone shaking me and saying "Wake up we are just about to land."

What!? How did I sleep through the entire journey – it was an eight hour trip? Staggering out of the airport with a huge dose of jetlag I found a taxi and went back home to plan how I was going to raise the money... and how much I actually needed to give this family some hope for the future.

Finally it was 7am! I had a disturbed night full of tossing and turning and now it was an appropriate time to get out of bed. After I got back to my apartment last night I had made arrangements to fundraise at the market today in Central London by selling apples. I got up and quickly got myself ready to go and set up the stall. Rushing out of the building I hopped into my small hatchback and sped away to the bustling square ready to make money.

Placing the last sign perfectly in place I was ready. The early birds had already started to arrive and bag up the bargains and soon the people were starting to fill the many jars with change in return for a crisp apple supplied by Michelle. Soon the jars started to overflow and I had to replace them with ice – cream containers, not as pretty but still doing the job well.

The day drew to an end and people started to disappear I began to pack up all my stuff and hauled it into my car. Driving away I was beginning to wonder how much money I had actually made by today, as it was really busy – apparently one of the busiest days for a long time.

As I finished counting the mountain of change I was gob-smacked because I had managed to raise the life-changing amount of £450! I was chuffed.

Now it was time for the final step, to present the sum to Raaghen and Dereask so they could finally be independent. Logging onto the travel agent's website I looked up Afghanistan flights. I slowly looked through each of the offers carefully and chose the best in value in a fortnight's time.

A fortnight later...As I hopped off of the aeroplane I dragged myself to the "hospital" and Raaghen & Dereask's bed with the cash behind my back.

"Hello, Heather!" Raaghen and Dereask exclaimed.

"Hi! I replied "I have a surprise for you."

"What?" Raaghen asked, unsure.

"This!" I said, revealing the cash from behind my back.

She was absolutely speechless her mouth open ready to catch flies.

"Is it all for me?" she stuttered. I nodded. After getting thank for over a thousand times and saying "Is that OK?" possible even more.

Walking away from that building made me realise the true value of life - giving, and what's wrong with it? Absolutely nothing. It makes you feel great, makes others better and it makes you believe that anything can happen.

It will be all right

By Madison Hart age 12

As I sit here, I look out over the crystal blue lake that's surrounded by beautiful green hills- some lined with gorgeous tall 'Christmas trees' and some just left empty with nothing but green grass. I have always loved the feeling of been open and free, with nothing but an open blue sky that isn't filled with a sight or sound such as a bird. It was just me, my thoughts and my hillside view.

I think about how my life used to be. Happy and filled with so many memories that I love to think back to, and laugh and smile about with not a care in the world. Memories of having the most amazing people around me, and the dreams of having a fantastic future doing what I wanted to do and being what some people would call successful. I wanted all of that.

It all started with one person. He was my life. I never thought that one person could mean so much to me- he was my best friend, my lover and soul-mate, well so I thought. We'd been through so much together, some things that neither of us would forget as long as we lived. As a teenager he turned my life around through tough times when I believed that my life wasn't worth living. Thanks to him I had my life. He saved me and I owed him all I had. We were young, but we knew that we were meant to be.

We hadn't been together for more than two years when he followed his dreams and went to war. He had wanted to be in the army ever since he was younger and I insisted that he followed his dream and went, making myself believe that I would be okay until he returned and followed another career path. At the age of 18, I didn't think that life would move so fast and that time would be limited. By the middle of the year, he left for training, where he soon found out he would very shortly be on the front line for eight months.

I never heard from him whilst he was away. He always believed that calling home or writing would make the pain more than it should be. Little did he know hearing his voice every now and then would have saved seconds, minutes, hours, days and months of gut wrenching pain of not knowing whether he was ok or not and whether he would ever return home. I needed him whether he needed me or not.

As much as I tried living my life, I wasn't the same person I used to be. Getting out of bed was a chore; I refused to go to university, let alone work. I just wouldn't leave the house. On his sixth month of being gone, I didn't leave the house for the whole month, I lived in my bedroom, leaving only to greet the Chinese delivery boy at the door and do the washing once a week. No-one saw me; I never answered my phone and the only person that bothered to come to my house to see me was my mother.

Today, sitting on a rock, in my beautiful hillside, is the first time that I've left my bedroom, let alone the house. It is the first day that I've had a long shower, actually bothering to brush my hair and put clothing on other than my pajamas. I felt like a normal person on the outside, but still the inside of me is breaking more and more, minute by minute.

I have taken a lot of consideration on what I am doing, and I think that this is the right path for me. Some may say it's stupid but it won't matter once I'm gone. No-one knows about this place, and I have no idea how my final letter will make it to my mother but here's hope that the letterbox I placed it in before I trudged down this huge hill will send it for me.

There is no-one here but me; there is not a sound of even a bird. The trees are still as the water. I'm ready to go, I clutch the necklace he gave me, walk up to the water, breathe in deeply and slowly walk into the lake until my head is underwater. It takes a while and whilst I want to push myself up and take a breath of air, I know I will suffer no more heartbreak and can watch over him from heaven and be with him, keeping him safe.

Just as I'm about to go, someone pulls me out of the frigid cold water. Believe it or not, it's him! We cry into each other's shoulders, just standing there not caring that the water was below freezing. He picks me up and drives me home, puts me to bed where I continue to cry my eyes out, even though I know everything is going to be all right. He makes me eat before we both go to sleep.

All I dream about was how I nearly had done it again, but now for the second time he had saved me from the dreaded grim reaper waiting for my soul.

Even though that was 60 years ago I still have the same dream over and over again. I wake up bawling my eyes out but he is always there for me and he whispers the same thing over and over again, "It will be all right, my darling, it will be all right."

The Sleepover

By Kathy Keane age12

Lola runs up and hugs me. We haven't seen each other in ages. I guess it's hard to have those long weekends together because we are at different schools now, but this weekend is going to be awesome. My parents are out of the house until Monday night. We go and put her stuff in the lounge and wave to my parents as their car races down the driveway. I turn to her and we both giggle. It's the first time we have the house to ourselves.

"What should we do first?" she asked me. I look around the living room thinking.

"How about we go see what movies I have?"

She nods and we go upstairs to the study. I open up the big wooden cupboards. About a hundred movies of every genre sit in there on the shelves. Her eyes wander straight for the sappy love stories while I prefer a good horror. She pulls out the Robert Downey Jr. movie *Only you*.

A smile creeps across her face as she looks at the young version of the actor she is obsessed about. I pull out possibly the best horror ever. *Ju on* is the scariest thing I've ever seen. I turn to her and hold up the movie. She looks at it and a look of disappointment appears on her face.

"Do we have to watch a scary movie? You know they're not my

thing."

"If we don't watch one then it's not a real sleepover," I say. She sighs and takes the movie out of my hand and looks at the cover.

"It does look interesting but, you do know that it's in Japanese, right?" I nod and she sighs again.

"Fine."

We head downstairs and decide what we should watch first. We finally agree to watch the girly movies first and the scary ones when it's dark.

Unfortunately we realize we are all out of lollies and pop corn.

"We can't be out already, we just started eating them," says Lola as her hand frantically searches the bottom of the jar on the off chance that some lollies were still there but had just decided to turn invisible. She puts the jar back on the table and glares at it.

"Come on, there's a dairy down the road. It'll only take us 15 minutes." I say getting up.

She gets off the couch smiling and nods. As we walk down the street the sun starts to disappear and with it goes the nice temperature. We rub our arms and watch our breath float up and vanish in to the air.

"Good God it's cold! I wish I brought a coat now. By the time we get to the dairy my fingers will have turned into icicles, "Lola says as she cups her hands and brings them up to her face to breathe warm air into them. We reach the dairy and I turn back to her and sigh.

"What's wrong?" she asks me. I shake my head.

"It's the Gremlin. I forgot he works on Fridays."

She looks down and curses at the dusty footpath. The Gremlin is a squat little old man whose eyes were as dark as black pudding. He is the meanest person in the entire town. The corners of his mouth constantly point downwards in a permanent frown as if the effort to smile once in a while was too hard to bear. Once he threw a friend of ours out of the shop. Some people say they saw our friend's feet leave the ground when the Gremlin had grabbed him by the scruff of the neck.

We need to think of what exactly we are going to get in there. " Popcorn, Lollies and what about a new tub of ice cream?"   She nods excitedly.

"Well we know our way around the store really well, so all we need to do is get in there, get served and get out. You ready?"   She looks at me jumps up and down to psyche herself up.

We enter the store, not making eye contact with the Gremlin and run straight for the isles. I dash to the lollies while Lola covers the frozen treats and the popcorn. We meet up at the checkout and I begin rummaging through my purse looking for the correct change. Lola puts all the stuff on the counter and I hand over my money. He counts the money and raises an eyebrow. He fixes his eyes on to mine. They glare at me in a menacing manner.

"You're 40cents short," he says with a hoarse tone. Lola and I look at each other and I swallow hard.

"Hang on, I must have another dollar or so left in my purse." I shove my hand inside my purse and grab for anything in reach. I feel something small and round and cold against my fingers. Seizing it I pull it out and release a long relieving sigh. I put the dollar on the counter. He's just about to give me my change when we grab our items and run for it.

"Keep the change!" I yell as we scramble out of the door way. We start to walk when we get closer to my house. As I unlock the front door I notice a black van with tinted windows parked across the street. Inside I can see in the front seats that there are two men with caps on and hoods pulled down low. The one in the passenger seat's hood turns to face me and even though I can't see his face I get the feeling he is looking me right in the eye, I shudder.

I open the door and we walk in. I follow Lola into the kitchen as she opens the popcorn and dumps it into a bowl. She does the same with the lollies and grabs two spoons for the ice cream.

"Wait before you press play, how scary is it?"

I roll my eyes. Sometimes I can't believe how much of a baby she is.

"The only way you'll find out is by watching it."

I press play and start the lesson in the art of scary movies.

We fall asleep after the movie, on the couch. In the middle of the night she hits me with the pillow and wakes me up giving me a fright.

"What?"

I turn to look at her. The room is lit up by the moon light coming through the blinds. Her eyes are wild with fear.

"There's someone trying to open the front the door," she whispers.

"God, that movie really scared you didn't?" I say with a giggle."Just go back to sleep, it was only a movie." I put my head back on my pillow and close my eyes but she shakes me.

"I'm serious."

"Who's there?" I call to the door. The handle stays still for a few moments and then starts to rattle more vigorously. I grab the fire poker and look out the window to see who it is. There parked outside my house is the black van. It sounds like they are trying to kick the door down now. I grab Lola and run up stairs and barricade us in my parent's room. I hear a loud crack from downstairs.

"They're inside." I say.

Lola starts to cry. I huddle close to her. The footsteps grow louder as they start to approach our furniture fortress. I grab the phone from the dressing table and dial 111.

"Please help us. My house is being broken into. There are two of us. My address is 37 Amelia Crescent. Please hurry."

I hang up and watch the door. There's a massive bang and our barricade starts to collapse. I look around the room to see if we can escape. Our only option is to climb out of the window. The door swings open and in burst four hooded figures. The two at the front are armed with baseball bats and golf clubs.

Quickly we crawl out onto the roof. It's raining outside which makes the roof slippery. We jump down onto the trampoline just as one of the gang members crawls out onto the roof. He grabs Lola by the hair and she starts to scream. I punch him in the face. I hear a crack as I break my knuckle. I wince and start to well up with tears.

The police turn up with an ambulance. The paramedics help us over to the ambulance where they fix up my hand. Some of the police run in my house, while some of them stay with their guns pointing at the person on the roof. One of the policemen, a family friend, walks over to me.

"Don't worry we called your parents. They should be here soon. How are you?"

"Fine. Thank you for ringing my parents," I say.

Maybe Lola and I will have a sleep over at her house next time.

Elizabeth

By Megan Knights

"You have got to understand," she said "That when you get old, dying is not the end of life but merely the beginning of a new journey." And with that she closed her eyes and I knew she was not going to open them again.

My vision was blurry and my cheeks were wet but I did not care. I stayed by her bedside for a long time, not taking my eyes off her just in case she stirred. But she did not.

*****

I think I better start from the beginning. My name is Elizabeth and I am 14 years old. It was two years ago when it all went wrong. It was October 1894. My mother and father could not afford a nice house and the winters were bitter. My mother, Ellen, did not work. She looked after the baby, the house and clothes. My father worked in the lumber business, cutting down trees. It was a hard job with very little pay but we made do with what we could.

One day my father was out working when the baby fell ill. Ma told me to call for the doctor. I put on my coat and ran outside on to the road, heading for the families doctors house. I soon got there panting and out of breath. I knocked on the door urgently. The maid answered. Before she could open her mouth I was gabbling away saying that I needed a doctor.

He was soon putting on his coat and heading for his carriage. We arrived home at the same time as Pa. He looked quizzically at the doctor then at my worried face. We went inside. Ma had moved the cot into the kitchen, near the fire. The baby was crying and sweating all over. The doctor stayed for ages but he could not save him. Ma was distraught. Little Elliott's funeral was a week after it happened.

A month later our next disaster struck. The news came through the town that there had been a big accident out at the lumber yard and three men had died. Pa never came home. The house seemed strangely quiet when I walked round it now. The house had to be sold and we moved into the country to live with our Grandmother. Our Grandmother was very old. She lived just outside the village.

*****

I went to my Grandmother's bedroom. "Hello Jessica," I said.
"Hello Miss Elizabeth."

Jessica looked after my Grandmother before we came and could not bear to leave her. She refused to call me Lizzie.

"Ma wants me to look after Grandmother for a while. You can stay if you want but you are welcome to go too."

"Thank you Miss Elizabeth but I'll stay here."

"How is Grandmother, where is she?"

"She is in the library. She sent me in here to tidy up."

I walked to the library and knocked on the door.

"Come in."

"Good afternoon Grandmother."

"Ahh how is my favourite Granddaughter?" she said putting down her book and leaning back in her armchair. She smiled at me as I walked towards her.

"Grandmother! What about Mary?" I said, shocked that she would say such a thing.

"Well she is my favourite too," she answered giggling slightly. I walked over to her chair, put a hand on her arm and laughed. Sometimes you just cannot help it with her.

We were in the library talking about her book. It was about a young girl who ran away and sailed on a boat to a place called New Zealand. It sounded like a magical place, full of beauty and adventure. Ma called through the hall.

"Dinner's ready!"

We went through into the dining room. The table was set and Mary was sitting there waiting. Grandmother and I sat down and Jess followed. The door opened and Ma came in pushing a trolley load of food. She pushed it over to the table and put a steaming plate full of delicious smelling food in front of each of us. We all had one sausage, one whole potato and a lot of chopped vegetables.

"Goodness Ma, what a feast!" Mary said.

"It is certainly something," Grandmother added.

When dinner was over I helped clear the table and then went off to bed. Mary and I shared a bedroom. We undressed and got into bed. I took my book from the bedside table and opened it up. In London I didn't go to school, only the boys and the rich girls went. Some had a private tutor but not having much money my sister and I didn't have an education. When my Grandmother heard that we could not read or write she began to teach us immediately and within a week we were taking classes with her. She had given us both a book to read in our quiet time. I really liked mine although the words were a bit hard. I read a whole page and then came to a word I did not know. I tried to sound it out like I had been taught but I could not do it so I put the book away, blew out my candle and went to sleep.

Grandmother decided that Mary and I were to go to school. It started the next day. At nine o clock I was at an unfamiliar desk surrounded by unfamiliar people in an unfamiliar room. Everyone knew everyone; I was the new strange girl. The teacher introduced herself as Miss Anderson, she was very nice.

All of Grandmothers tutoring paid off for although I was not the brightest student, I could understand everything the class debated. We practiced spelling and mathematics, geography and vocabulary, and once we were finished with the text book work, we were permitted to draw or paint what we liked.

At the end of the day Miss Anderson told us that we were to revise what we had learnt that day and also that we were to finish a piece of artwork at home.

"I will give you two weeks," she announced.

We all went home excited over this new assignment. When I got home I ran straight through to Grandmother to tell her all about my day. Once I had finished she smiled and clapped her hands together. At once I knew I wanted to draw my Grandmother.

"It is perfect!" I exclaimed. "Oh please allow me to draw you Grandmother, please!"

She smiled and nodded her head.

"All right dear," she said.

I ran to get my sketch pad and colouring pencils from my satchel which I had dropped off in my room on the way to Grandmother's room. I raced back and sat down on the floor.

Grandmother had posed with one hand on her cheek, elbow propped up on the table beside her armchair. I started with the surroundings around her, too scared to look directly at my Grandmother. Slowly I worked up the courage to start drawing Grandmother herself. As I was drawing I slowly found myself begin to enjoy myself. I began to ease into the drawing, keeping my eyes focused on Grandmother, hardly looking at my sketchpad. I finished the basic outline of the portrait and then stopped.

"Let me have a look dearie," Grandmother said.

Instantly shy I turned it around to face her. She gasped.

"It is very good! Elizabeth you have a talent!"

"Thank you Grandmother."

I knew she was right and I felt very pleased with myself. Grandmother left the room but I stayed where I was on the floor adding the detail and colour of the surroundings. I tried to get the light and shade of each object exactly right. They looked real on the page, like I could reach out and grab them at any moment and they would be there for me to feel in my hand. When I had done I put the sketch book on the table and went to dinner.

When I woke up the next morning I knew immediately that something was wrong. The house was silent, eerie. I got up and walked through to the kitchen. There was Jessica tears streaming down her cheeks, packing her bag.

"Jess!" I cried, "You are not leaving are you?"

"Yes Miss Elizabeth, I must. I have to go."

Jess was crying so much she could barely speak. She left the kitchen and walked through to the library. Mother was there silently crying and looking at the drawing I had left on the table from yesterday. She and Jessica hugged and Mother gave her an envelope. They hugged once more. Then Jess turned and left and left the house forever. We never saw her again.

Mother said I was not to go to school today. Neither was Mary. Grandmother was ill, very ill, dying in fact. The doctor said there was very little chance of recovery and all we could do was pray. It was dinner time and I was nursing Grandmother while Mary and Ma prepared the meal. Grandmother opened her eyes and I mopped her forehead.

"Hello my favourite Grandchild," she said weakly.

"Oh Grandmother!" I cried, breaking down at the sound of her weak croaky voice. It broke my heart to see her lying there so frail and helpless, like a feather could break her. "You are not going to die are you?"

Then my Grandmother took my hand in hers, looked me in the eye and said weakly but seriously.

"You've got to understand," she said "that when you get old, dying is not the end of life but merely the beginning of a new journey." And with that she closed her eyes and I knew she wasn't going to open them again.

My vision was blurry and my cheeks were wet but I didn't care. I stayed by her bedside for a long time, not taking my eyes off her just in case she stirred. But she didn't. Mother knocked on the door and gently opened it. She looked at me, saw the tear stained cheeks and knew straight away what I had not told her. No words were said as she quickly crossed the room and pulled me into a hug both of us crying softly. We stayed like that for a long time. Eventually we pulled apart.

"I never got to finish my drawing," I sobbed.

And that was the end. We lived on in that house. I found a nice man, married and had three children. Mary stayed a maid, looking after Ma in her old age. I took the unfinished drawing with me when I moved. I never tried to finish it; it stayed a detailed background and a rough outline of my Grandmother, sitting in her favourite chair in the library leaning on the table, smiling slightly her features barely drawn in.

I continued drawing, my husband, my children, my children's children and even full family portraits if I could get the little ones to sit still for long enough. But nothing is as good as my first and only picture of my hero, my Grandmother. And that is my story of many tragedies and smiles but mainly the story of my lovely, kind hearted and amazing Grandmother.

Five years lost

By Jason Liu age 12

2019 was a world of chaos.

My alarm clock went off. I seemed to just get to sleep after hours of tossing and turning trying to get comfortable. After thirty seconds of beeping, I finally gathered enough strength to push a single button to stop the noise. I hadn't had a goodnight's sleep in five years, ever since the infection arrived.

My name is Jonathan Miles and I am thirty two years old. I had a wife called Emily and two kids called Michal and Brent but they are gone. Either, infected, dead, or alive out there is the unsafe world. I miss them terribly. I am and intend to stay as a helicopter pilot in the military.

Living on a small island base off the coast of infected England, this was where my family and I got split up on a holiday when virus M121 broke and caused havoc. These small island bases are scattered all over the world to control the seas and the coastlines. The infected and bandits control the mainland. Our daily helicopter round involves scanning the coastline for any bandits, survivors and any new groups of infected and check on the main hordes of infected, numbering around 20,000 to 80,000 at our last count. Our first round today was to pick up a group of survivors that radioed for help. In case it was a trap, we had two Reaper UCAV (unmanned combat air vehicle) giving us a heads up on locations of enemies and give us close air support.

I was very quiet flying to the rendezvous, listening to the constant drone of the engines. Usually there are bandits firing guns at us but today was suspiciously quiet. After I handed the controls to my co-pilot, I walked back to the cargo bay where my squad was waiting to be dropped off at the rendezvous. They were sitting with a 50cal Machine gun Humvee, greedily waiting to be dropped off.

I told my crew that we were five minutes to the rendezvous, to gear up and get ready to leave to pick up the survivors. The rendezvous was in the bush so it was inaccessible by air. We tried to talk the survivors in to leaving the bush so it was accessible by air but they replied with, "We have an injured person, sir!"

That comment made us more suspicious. It was as if they "wanted" to stay in the bush with plenty places to hide, making an ambush easy. We landed smoothly on the edge of the bush. We opened the cargo bay door and drove outside in to the wilderness. As soon as we cleared the helicopter, it took off without saying a goodbye. The pilots were warned that the survivors wanted to steal our multimillion dollar helicopter.

As we set off, I contacted the crew flying the reaper drones and to check if there was any movement ahead of our location. Their reply was, "Negative sir! Only a couple of walkers ahead but you can handle that. Don't worry; we'll warn you if anything suspicious comes within one kilometre of you guys! Good luck!"

I turned off my radio with a sinking feeling in my stomach. I was nervous. I never thought of dying out here doing my job as a helicopter pilot, I mean that you'd think that you'd just fly huge metal beasts. Little did I know that when I was that I was promoted to sergeant and I would have to command my own squad and kill and save people. I never intended to actually be a frontline soldier in the army. Well, life's unfair is it not?

As we entered the bush, it reminded me of my home town in New Zealand called Palmerston North. A few kilometers away there was a gorge track and my dad and I used to hike for hours on end in the bush. Those were the good times. I wondered if the track was still there. I heard that New Zealand was a neutral (not infected) country. I continued thinking about the past until I heard a rude interruption to the silence.

"Nova 6! Do you copy? I repeat, Nova 6 do you copy? This is reaper leader! Over."

It was my radio.

"This is Nova 6; I copy you loud and clear. What do you wa…"

"There are bogies (bad guys) on your six (back)!!!!! We are engaging!!!"

I urgently told my drive to speed up.

"There are bogies on our tail" I shouted to my crew as I clambered up into the 50cal. Turret. I looked through the crosshairs of the gun sight and aimed at a Toyota Hilux with a group of people firing all sorts of guns at us. Just as I was about to take my shot, the vehicle burst into flames and the screams of the men echoing in between the trees.

"Target destroyed!" called my radio. But there were more bandits to come, riding on motor bikes, cars, and even foot soldiers. It would take a while for them to catch up! I kept spraying them with fifty calibre bullets but they continued coming from out of the bushes.

I knew that the rendezvous was coming but I had no idea what to do. In the end, we decided that we would call in the reapers to fire all of their missiles at the targets one hundred metres from the rendezvous. Then we would stop and pick up the survivors if there were any and evacuate the area and rendezvous with the helicopter and get the hell out of here! I wasn't sure about the plan that Doug the driver suggested but everyone agreed. One hundred meters out, the reapers fired all of their missiles managing to kill most of the pursuers. A few were left but I finished them off with the 50cal. As the survivors came into view, I saw three persons standing outside a hut, one lady and two kids.

They looked all too familiar as I glanced at them. I hopped out of the Humvee and explained the situation to them. I told them to get into the Humvee and hold on. One kid had a badly sprained ankle like they said on the radio. After the kids climbed in without much problem, the woman awkwardly glanced back at me and said, "Jonathan?"
"Emily?" I replied out of the blue.
Suddenly it all came back to me! It was Emily, my long gone wife and kids! I heard moans and groans from a group of infected behind.
"How did you get... We have to go!"
I got in with my wife and drove away from the infected as fast as we could.

"Is it really you?"

"Yes, it really is me my love."

I hugged her and the kids in the first time in five years. It felt good to be with my family. Almost too good, as we didn't realize we were being chased! Not again! I climbed up into my spot and did my job as well as I could before I ran out of ammo. I never thought of running out of ammunition but I guess I had wasted a lot just spraying the bandits. Now we were in real trouble with many enemies on our tail and no suppressing fire.

"Do you have anything to do with this?"I asked Emily sternly.

"No! These attacks are usual!" she replied with truth in her tone.

Suddenly, out of the blue popped a helicopter and it started to fire rockets towards us. I braced for impact but all I felt was a whoosh of heat and an explosion. It was here to help and pick us up from hell. The helicopter raced ahead and landed with its bay door open.

"Nova 6! This is Boomstick, we are here to pick you up from this hell hole, over!" croaked the radio.

We drove up the bay door ramp and skidded to a stop. Almost as soon as the back set of wheels hit the ramp, we were airborne.

"Well that was a hell of a day!" called one of my crew who was manning a gun turret.

I stared out into the vast blue ocean from the open bay door as we were on our way back to base. I was soon joined by Emily, Michal and Brent and we hugged hard and long, hoping that we would never need to part ever again.

Slender man

By Thomas Mitchell age 12

I am running to Granny's house with the pink iced slice in my basket. I see the figure of Slender Man, he's chasing me. His blood thirsty mouth is dripping saliva and I can hear the beating of the ground as he approaches. My heart is pounding as I hear the screams in his voice. I thread myself through the dark, misty trees trying to lose him. As I look behind, no one is in sight so it did it work and I am safe.

I hear a sound. I can't be sure. I look up and I see, RUN!!! I can feel the cold, slimy tentacles reaching out for me. The foggy face of Slender Man shows no mercy, so I run for my life. I suddenly come to a halt and Slender Man hits the tree behind me. The worn soles of my shoes skid along the dry dirt like a plane on the tarmac. I scramble to get back up and head for Granny's.

His dislocated neck turns to look at me, Arrrrrrr!! I scramble up the nearest tree to hide from the almighty Slender. As I catch my breath I see him looking for me. I feel in my pockets but they are empty. I look. Is it true? I see a tree hut with a knife, bow and arrows. The only thing in my way is him, he's standing below the tree. I can only get to the tree by silently swinging through the tree tops. I run and jump like an owl swooping in the pitch black sky. I land with a bang as Slender Man scans the area and I grab the items that I saw from my perch up in the tree.

I load and shoot the only arrow I have then I jump and land on the ground with knife in hand. With a hand behind his head the arrow was caught at full speed. This is when I knew my mistake had been made.

Slender Man is deathless. His tentacles wrap around my legs and I see the foggy face of Slender once again.

Slender may be deathless but it's worth a try with the knife. The cold blade cut through the tentacles weeping warm black blood on to my fear felt skin. The screams of Slender are heard for 1000miles. I slip from the cold dark fingers of death once again when I think my life is over. The only thing that is keeping me alive is the slick fast thinking of my brain keeping me from certain death.

I run faster and faster as the body of Slender is behind me. He's getting so close to me now, one false step is certain death. Once again I try to escape. I slide under a pile of nearby leaves to catch my breath. That attack back there was too close, next time I have to keep a distance away.

As my eyes emerge from the soggy, slime covered leaves, I wonder where could he be now? My arms pull my body out of the dirty, dark leaves for a closer look. I wander around, Slender is nowhere in sight. I have questions running through my mind. Have I finally got away, has he finally given up on chasing me? Where am I? I wander in the direction of granny's house not knowing where the mighty Slender might be seen

As I walk further I can see a foggy mist over Granny's house. I've made it I think as my swift shoes flick up the gravel as I run to the house of my grandmother. My shaking hands reach up and touch the bronze incrusted knocker that lies in the centre of the door. I am led to believe that I am safe as I hear the words.

"Come in dear," from my grandmother's soft voice.

I walk in onto the polished floor boards leading to the bedroom where my grandmother lies. I see her on the bed and for some reason she looks different. A hair cut or maybe plastic surgery, no it must just be me. I climb up onto the feather filled, flower decorated quilt. As I pass the slice over I pause and shred the masking covering my granny's face. She laughs as I see her real face underneath. It was all a joke. She knew I had read the book Red Riding Hood and thought it would be funny to dress up like the wolf in the story.

As I walk to the cupboard and open it for fun, I see HIM. Nooooo! I thought he was gone and now I'm trapped, I am going to die. Before I can even think about running, the cold black vines that are Slender's tentacles wrap around my neck and strangle me cold dead. I am dead...

-

My Hero

By Gabriell Ou age 12

Every day when I wake up I wonder why I am here. Every time I look in the mirror I know nothing has changed overnight. Wherever I go, whenever people see me I get the same response. It's neither my fault nor theirs. I'm just a normal kid, but normal kids don't make other normal kids run away or point and stare. I won't describe my face because whatever you're thinking, it's probably worse.

I absolutely hate school. I'm not sure why I even need to go. Most the kids in my neighbourhood usually drop out by my age and go work with their fathers. However the orphanage makes us go. If we even think about ditching school it's a night in the lonely, murky and grubby attic. What the orphanage feeds us is ghastly too: corned beef, bread, mutton and the occasional potato. Always I am hungry afterwards too; though this mostly because I am slow at eating due to the surgery I had when I was born, to my palate, which means I can only eat with my front teeth.

So every single day after a pitiful meal, I drag myself off to the dreaded school. They tease me and call me names because of my face however, what hurts the most is when they talk about how my parents did not want me. My social worker tells me to ignore them, but how can I ignore them when they are laughing right in my face? I have become used to it, but every night I still pray that at least one person can love me.

I wish that I could have a Dad to play with, to tell me that the bullies are wrong. In the playground I see the boys with their fathers telling them how much they love each other; I see how the boys boast about their father's, saying that they want to be just like them, that they are their hero. Then I look around me, where is my Dad? Why is he not here? What did I do to deserve this? I always cry when I think about this.

On my way back from school I just cannot take the truth anymore. I have no friends, no family, no one loves me. Their glaring faces kept coming back to me, their words whirling in my head like a carousel. Zombie boy, unwanted, abandoned, deformed. The words beat in my heart with venomous power. Breaking my defenses and shattering my spirit. I have kept that white flag within me for so long, but now I will let it flutter in the wind......

Changing the route I start walking sorrowfully along the path towards the river. A big beautiful moon perches above the mountains and leaves rustle with the soft breeze. An old willow is standing crooked by the river and reaching towards the sky. Tears flow down my face, as easy as the river flows itself. I crawl up the tall willow and just sit there for a long time, thinking about everything that has happened in my life; school, the orphanage and my parents leaving me.

I sit longer wishing that my father would just pop up and tell me that we are going home, to say he is sorry and would be my hero. This is just my own imagination but the picture was so vivid in my mind.

The moon starts to fade away. I think it is time. I take one more look before I fall into eternity. Before I can hesitate I jump!

The world slows down around me, my body twisting gracefully in the air. I close my eyes and cross my arms over my chest, thinking it is my last moment. However the splash breaking the silence chooses differently...

Water is rushing over my head. At first I do not believe where I am, but then I abruptly sit up. It is taking a while to sink in, but I am alive! I feel alive! All those terrible words were washed away and replaced with new words like *Bravery, Courage and Integrity.* I feel different, a new person, as if my inner self has been reborn. I do not need my father back. He does not love me and he does not care about me or want to be my hero.

<u>I am my own hero!</u>

Ambush

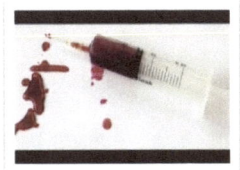

By Jack Pinder age12

I'm tired, I'm hungry, I'm sore and I'm thirsty.

The road stretches before me, I'm waiting. The German outpost is 5km south. With nothing but the clothes on my back and what I have found, I'm stranded in a cross-fire between the Germans and the French. The French are getting beaten easily.

I am a scavenger taking anything I can from the Germans. Guns, food, anything from jam to gas masks. I'm going to die and when I do, I'm going take out as many Germans as I can. I'm training myself; hunting and running whenever I can. Germans are cowards; they hide behind their guns and just shoot people dead.   I have blonde hair and blue eyes, so if I went in as a normal citizen with no home the Germans might take me in as a soldier. I hate Germans because the only thing I can remember is a German scientist in a white lab coat sticking a massive needle into my arm. I step onto the road and start running, south.

Today I could die.

The German outpost is a simple jog from where I was standing. I slow to a walk. As I near the outpost a German soldier steps out holding a gun, a M16. I walk up to the guard, worry probably plastered all over my face. The German opens his mouth and a low rough voice says "I.D?" in German.

"Bones."

I hadn't thought about that. The German seeing the shock on my face starts to lift the gun. My mind goes on auto pilot I step in closing the couple meters gap, ducking under the gun I land a few light jabs into his midsection knocking him back a couple of steps. He might be a soldier but it looks like he's had too many pies and no exercise.

The German lifts his gun again, anger burning bright in his eyes, this time he wouldn't miss, this time I would die. The German moved slowly forward, I knew it was no use. His hand tightens on the trigger. I look away. A gunshot sounds, one solitary shot, not the ripping sound of a M16. I look up, the German lies on the ground, dead. A man and a woman step out of the shadows, the woman holding a hunting rifle, both with hardened looks on their faces. The man speaks in rough English.

"Boy, your name?"

"Bones."

I just realised, I don't know my own name, **I don't know my own name.**

"I don't know," I manage to spit of my mouth. "I don't know."

The man narrows his eyes. Distrust.

"Come with us," an order.

The pair turned and melted in to the shadows, I follow. I don't exactly trust them but they are the only thing I have. When I catch up the man is holding two seven inch knifes one in one hand and the other on hilt first pointing at me, offering me the knife. I take the knife and stick it into my belt within easy reach. Our trio makes its way through the shrubbery. A bullet hits the man in the head making him fall over from the impact. The woman rips around and then suddenly drops to the ground, dead. A sharp pain hits my leg making me drop to the ground, black is on the edges on my vision. Just as I black out I see German soldiers coming through the under bush...

I wake up with a burning thirst in the back of my throat. My arms are lying limp in front of me shackled to the wall behind me. There is a German soldier in front of me.

"He's awake," he says calmly to the person leaning on the wall, his back turned to me. He turns around, his face shocked me, it was blonde with blue eyes, and it would have been handsome if not for the massive scar that ran from the right side of his lip to his temple, narrowly missing his left eye. His face was always grinning as the result. He walks slowly towards me. He stabs something into the side of my arm; I somehow can't move to stop him.

THE HERO DOG

By Flint Rogers age 11

My heart is pounding as I sprint up the wobbly stairs to the top storey of the abandoned windmill. The windmill creaks as I jump up the final step and look around desperately for a form of weapon. A pitch fork catches my eye. I leap forward and snatch it, holding it so tightly that my knuckles turn white from the pressure and fear.

Two drooling zombies come creeping up the staircase and lumber towards me. I leap into battle and stab the pitch fork into the first zombie, it staggers round the room until it approaches the window. I give it an almighty shove and it topples out. The second zombie is advancing at a crawl then suddenly it jumps up at me and engages in hand-to-hand combat. I duck and swerve until it gives out and I let go a mighty punch that sends him flying into space. I cannot relax because I know there will be more.

The glowing moon is my only form of light until a shadowy figure cast darkness over the room.

"Who's there?" I cry.

"Who's there yourself you creeping zombie filth!" comes my reply. An elderly gentleman steps forward fitted from head to toe in some sort of anti-radiation suit welding a ferocious looking six-shooter.

He lets loose a volley of shots which all but one fail to reach their target. I stagger to the ground as my killer approaches, blood pouring from my wound.

"Oh my goodness gracious me. You're not a zombie. Stinking creatures," he replies, only much more gently this time.

"You had better follow me back to the R.S.H.N.4."

"Raayshahaanafour?"

"R.S.H.N.4. Resistance Safe House Number 4."

"You mean there are more?"

"What?"

"Resistance, are there more humans, like not zombies."

"Ohh, well there used to be more but…"

"Urgghh," I interrupt. I make some more gurgling noises and pass out.

I awake in a crisp white bed with a lean black and white dog resting on my lap. I try to get up but my bullet wound does not allow me to. From now on my wounds are in charge. I go back to sleep and wake later and the dog is gone, however a plump nurse walks in. She sees me and gives me a cheerful smile.

"Well hullo there, you must be the new recruit," she tells me.

"Hi, I'm Jake, I'm not a new recruit although I can fight."

"Excellent, allow me to help you get up and have a look around the place."

"OK."

We step outside into a white corridor and walk until we come to a beautiful courtyard. I sit down on a bench overgrown with lush ivy glistening with the sun, and listen to the sound of birds singing. I think back over the past few days and recall how the horrific zombie invasion even started in the first place. 'How *did* it start?' I wonder to myself. It was just a big mystery, nobody knew how it started or how to stop it.

My thoughts are interrupted when a scientist in a lab coat bursts through a pair of doors and into the courtyard shouting.

"I've done it. I know how to defeat the zombies, I did it, we're saved. Yippee. We're gonna live. Hooray."

He steps towards me menacingly. Strange, the nurse has disappeared.

"Well, do you know the best way of getting rid of zombie's kiddo?"

"No sir," I answer warily.

"Well too bad because we don't want to tell you our secret."

"Our?"

"Yes, our secret, ZOMBIES ATTACK!"

Zombies spring out of their hiding places and begin to close in on me. The old man and the plump nurse and everyone else in the so called resistance were zombies all along. Well, I definitely don't have any allies here, but suddenly the dog which was sitting on my lap stands valiantly by my side.

"GRRRRR!"

The dog takes a step back and suddenly bounds forward into the crowd of rotten flesh and begins a furious attack. Zombie after zombie fall to the dog's brave attacks. A zombie catches hold of the dog's tail and another grabs the front left hand paw. It's time for me to step in. I dash for the zombies and let loose some powerful punches as they topple to the ground. I look up, and there are no more zombies.

"Reckon we make a good team, eh."

"Rrrooooff!"

"Hmmmmm… I think I'll call you Molly."

"Rrrooooff."

"Molly, the hero dog."

Books by Rangitawa Publishing.

<u>Fiction</u>

The Case of the Distant Relative - Jill Darragh
Creating Infinity - Jill Darragh
The Rangitawa Collection of short stories 2013 – various New Zealand authors.

<u>Non Fiction and poetry.</u>

Haiku and Humour – international poetry.
By Invitation - Jill Darragh

<u>Children's Fiction.</u>

Milly Feather – Jill Darragh
Childrenz One – various New Zealand authors
Childrenz Two -- various New Zealand authors

www.ingramcontent.com/pod-product-compliance
Lightning Source LLC
Chambersburg PA
CBHW040742250626
47164CB00001BA/11

* 9 7 8 0 9 9 4 1 0 8 8 0 7 *